PJ MASKS

PJ MASKS SAVE THE EARTH!

Simon Spotlight

New York London Toronto Sydney New Delhi

SIMON SPOTLIGHT
An imprint of Simon & Schuster Children's Publishing Division
New York   London   Toronto   Sydney   New Delhi
1230 Avenue of the Americas, New York, New York 10020
This Simon Spotlight edition March 2021

For information about special discounts for bulk purchases, please contact Simon & Schuster Special Sales at 1-866-506-1949 or business@simonandschuster.com.
Manufactured in the United States of America 0121 LAK
2 4 6 8 10 9 7 5 3 1
ISBN 978-1-5344-7974-6
ISBN 978-1-5344-7975-3 (eBook)

Greg, Connor, and Amaya are walking home from school when they notice something wrong. "What is that smell?" Connor asks. "Whatever it is, it sure is awful," Greg replies.

All the garbage cans in the city have been knocked over, leaving a smelly mess everywhere. There is even garbage scattered over the playground.

"Whoever did this is hurting the Earth," Amaya says. "We need to stop them!"

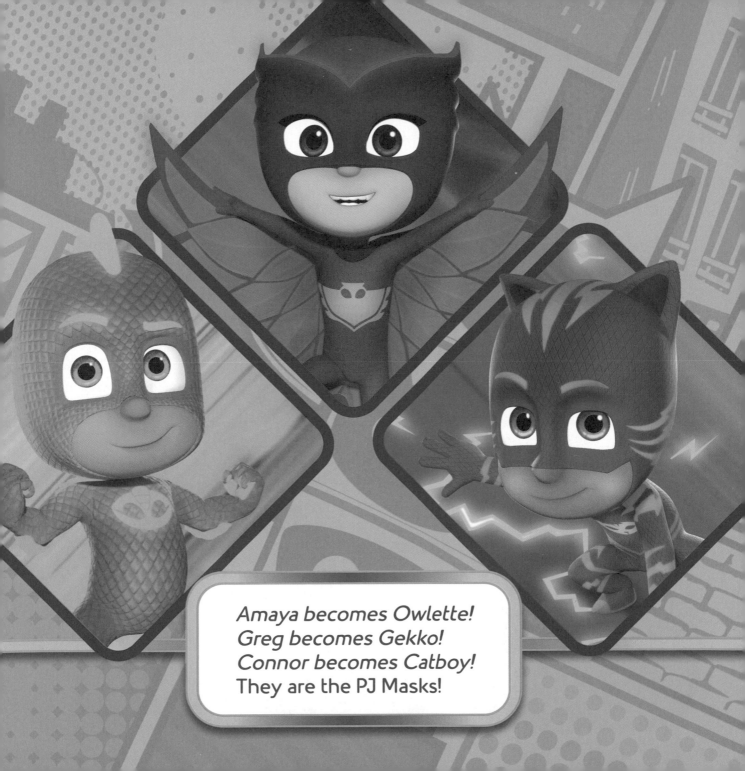

Amaya becomes Owlette!
Greg becomes Gekko!
Connor becomes Catboy!
They are the PJ Masks!

The garbage can outside Gekko's house has been knocked over too. Owlette gets closer to see if she can find any clues.

"Yuck!" Catboy says. "I'm staying away. I hate anything that smells bad."

Next, the PJ Masks head out into the city streets. Food scraps, old wrappers, and other trash are littered everywhere. "I can't stand the smell anymore!" Catboy says. "Let's go to HQ."

The PJ Masks head over to HQ to gather more information. PJ Robot notices someone on the Picture Player. It is Armadylan!

"But Armadylan is not a baddie," Gekko says. "Why would he litter?"

There is only one way to find out. The PJ Masks jump into the Gekko-Mobile and ride off into the night.

The smell of garbage has gotten even worse.

The PJ Masks find Armadylan by the playground. "Hey, guys!" Armadylan says. "I was just about to start my new training routine. I thought of it all by myself. Do you want to watch me?"

Before the PJ Masks can answer, Armadylan curls into a ball and takes off.

"Watch out!" Catboy cries, but Armadylan can't hear anything. He picks up speed, bounces off a garbage can, and rolls onto the city streets.

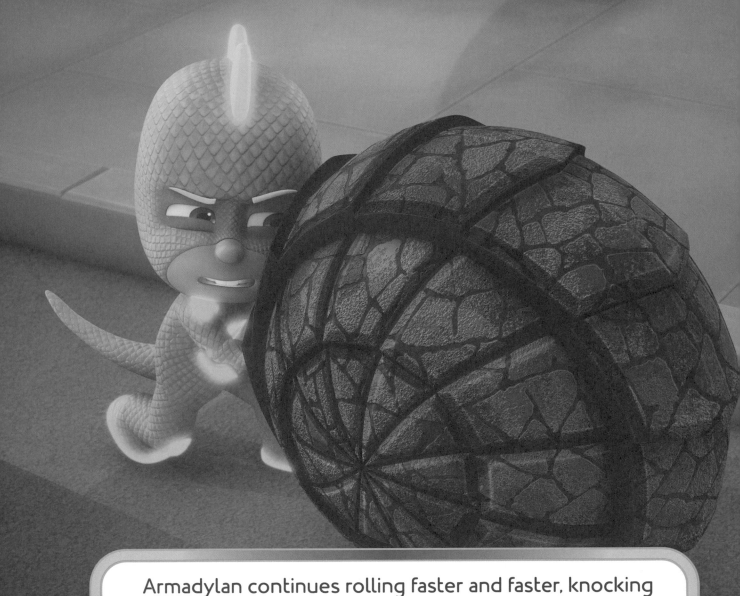

Armadylan continues rolling faster and faster, knocking into garbage cans and recycling bins on the sidewalk.

Gekko jumps into Armadylan's path. "Super Gekko Muscles!" he says, stopping Armadylan before he can cause any more damage.

"Hey! Why did you stop me?" Armadylan asks. "I was just getting warmed up. Real heroes get stronger by practicing their powers."

"Every time you roll into a can, you knock it over. You're littering everywhere, and the whole city stinks!" Catboy says.

Armadylan shrugs. He doesn't know why the PJ Masks are making such a big deal.

"It is important to practice your powers to get stronger," Owlette says. "But it's not okay to hurt the Earth while you're doing it."

Armadylan scratches his head. "Sorry about knocking the cans over," he says. "I didn't know that littering was such a big deal. I'll think of another training routine that helps me get stronger and protects the Earth at the same time."

The PJ Masks help Armadylan clean up his mess. Owlette uses her Owl Wing Wind to gather the garbage into one place. Gekko and Armadylan work together to carry it away.

Catboy is not happy about cleaning up. He still hates the smell of garbage and doesn't want to get his hands dirty, either.

"We have so much to clean!" Owlette says.

"If we all work together, we can get it done before morning," adds Gekko.

But Catboy is done cleaning tonight. He leaves his friends and goes back to HQ alone.

After a while, Owlette, Gekko, and Armadylan start to get tired. It is almost time for them to go home, but there is still a lot of garbage left to pick up.

"Everyone throws away too much stuff," Owlette complains. "We'll never finish cleaning up before daytime!"

Back at HQ, Catboy watches his friends working hard on the Picture Player. He realizes that if he really wants to save the Earth, he has to pitch in. His friends can't do it alone. "It's time to be a hero!" he shouts.

"Super Cat Speed!" Catboy says, zipping through the city to pick up the rest of the garbage. He uses his Super Cat Stripes to lasso the bins that were knocked over and put them right-side up.

With Catboy's help, the PJ Masks and Armadylan are able to clean up the city before nighttime is over. The sidewalks are clean, the cans and bins are all in their places, and it doesn't smell bad anymore.

"Thank you for helping," Gekko says to Catboy. "Real heroes protect the Earth," Catboy replies. "And they also work together!"